Guess Who?

T he doorbell rang and I came downstairs to open it. And there was Grandpa."

"Now I know you're lying!" snorted my mother, as if she was happy to catch me at it. "I spoke to my dad on the phone a few hours ago and he was still in Hawaii."

Quietly, I said, "No, I mean my other grandpa. The one who's in Woodmere Cemetery. I didn't recognize him at first, because he was just a skeleton. He was poking a bone that used to be his finger into the bell."

Shivers and Shakes

Larry Weinberg

illustrated by Mia Tavonatti

Troll

Library of Congress Cataloging-in-Publication Data

Weinberg, Larry.
   Shivers & shakes / by Larry Weinberg; illustrated by Mia
Tavonatti.
      p.   cm.
     Summary: A collection of twelve scary stories in which people come
back from the dead, two quarreling brothers turn into animals, and
other strange things occur.
    ISBN 0-8167-7606-7 (pbk.)
    1. Horror tales, American.   2. Children's stories, American.
[1. Horror stories.   2. Short stories.]   I. Tavonatti, Mia, ill.
II. Title.   III. Title: Shivers and shakes.
PZ7.W4362Sh   1994
[FIC]—dc20   93-24445

This edition published in 2002.

Text copyright © 1994 by Larry Weinberg.
Illustrations copyright © 1994 by Troll Communications L.L.C.

Printed in Canada.

10 9 8 7 6 5 4 3

TABLE OF CONTENTS

THE GHOST AT THE WINDOW

The great blizzard of 1993 began on Peter's birthday. Most of his friends called to say they couldn't come to his party, but his three greatest pals came over with their sleeping bags before the snow got too heavy.

The boys stuffed themselves with enough food and

cake for twelve kids. Then they played and watched videos until the wind outside grew to hurricane force and all the electricity went out.

When it was time for bed, the four friends bedded down by the fireplace. They lay on their sides, watching the logs burn and listening to the wind.

"It's getting spooky out there," murmured Gonzo (a name he preferred to Sidney).

"Definitely time for scary stories," declared Billy. "But not those old ones we've heard a thousand times. Let's make up our own."

"I'm not any good at imagining stuff," groaned Jonathan. "Somebody else go first."

"Okay, I will," said Peter, who already had the ghost of an idea.

"This story happened right here in Salem," he began. "In fact, it happened in this very house, which was built during the time of the Puritans. Of course it was a smaller place then—just this one room. But one room was enough, because the only person who lived here was a strange old woman who had eyes that never blinked. The farmers all said she was a witch who had put the evil eye on them. They blamed her when their cows took sick and died. So one day they tied her to a tree and burned her alive. It was to save her soul, they said. But she cursed them with her screams."

"I don't think I like this story," said Jonathan, who was the youngest at the party. "Why don't we just tell some of the old stories we know already?"

"Hey, cover your ears if you're afraid to listen," cried Gonzo.

Peter lowered his voice mysteriously and went on. "Well, the Puritans were wrong about the old woman. She wasn't a witch. But what they did to her was so unfair that she couldn't rest easy in her grave. Her ghost wanted to go home. So every night she rose up from the ground where they'd thrown her ashes. Then she tried to come back here—to this house. This room."

"Are you sure you're making this up?" Jonathan interrupted nervously.

"Maybe I am, and maybe I'm not," said Peter. Slowly he gazed from face to face. Then he went on. "But here's the catch. The people who bought the house after the old lady died really *were* witches. They spread an invisible mist around the house that kept it safe from spirits of the dead. So each time the ghost came to the house she couldn't break through the mist. All she could do was scratch the windows and howl to be let in. Howl like that wind we're hearing outside right now. And scratch. And scratch. And scratch . . ."

"Peter, stop doing that!" Jonathan cried.

"Doing what?" he asked innocently.

"You're scratching on something to scare me."

"No, I'm not." Peter held up his hands to prove it.

"Then one of you other guys is doing it."

Gonzo and Billy lifted their hands also.

"It's coming from that window!" gasped Jonathan. He dove into his sleeping bag.

"Will you please just *relax,*" snorted Peter. He was sorry he'd ever started the tale. "That's just some branch blowing against the glass. Here, I'll show you."

Going over to the curtain that covered the big bay window, he tugged on the cord that made it draw back. He stood to the side while it opened up, not even bothering to look for himself.

"You satisfied?" he asked Jonathan. But now all three of his friends were trembling. Their eyes bulged and they pointed behind him.

Peter thought that they were trying to have a little fun with him. Okay, he could be a good sport. With a grin on his face he turned around. And then he saw her!

She was an old woman. She wore a long black coat and a little black fur hat. She was covered with snow. And her face was pressed against the glass as if she was begging them to let her in. Again and again her long fingernails scratched against the window.

"It's the ghost!" cried Jonathan. He jumped to his feet and ran from the playroom, screaming to be taken home.

Peter's father and mother hurried out of their bedroom to see what was the matter. They were shivering with cold because the heat had gone off. And they were in absolutely no mood for any nonsense.

"Who hit you?" Mr. Cabot demanded.

"Nobody hit him, Dad. We saw a ghost at the window!"

"I don't care about the storm," Jonathan bellowed. "I wanna go home before she gets in!"

"There aren't any ghosts," declared Mr. Cabot, glaring at the older children. "It's easy to start seeing things when you're scared."

"But, Dad," cried Peter. "This was real!"

"Not another word!" commanded his mother. She turned to her husband. "What is it with boys? Why do they do these things to each other?"

"But, Mom," cried Peter. "We opened the curtain and there she was! Come and see for yourself!"

When Mrs. Cabot stamped her foot it meant she was really angry. "Look, there's no heat in this house! The four of you have that fire to keep you warm. So if you don't mind, *we* would like to get back under all our covers. Now you kids march right back in there and close that curtain and go to sleep. Do you all hear me?"

There was nothing the boys could do but turn around and shut their eyes tight so that they wouldn't have to look at the window. Peter walked backward to the curtain and pulled it closed. Then they all climbed into their sleeping bags and tried to think of other things. After a while their hearts stopped fluttering. And one by one, they all fell asleep.

None of them woke up until late the next morning when the delicious smell of hot cocoa drifted in from the kitchen. The lights were working. Heat was coming through the baseboard in the floor. And everything felt so cheery that Peter thought, *Boy, did I ever tell a story! Mom and Dad must have been right. We only imagined we saw a ghost in the window. Besides, what self-respecting ghost is going to hang around in the daytime?*

Aloud he said, "I wonder how much snow there is outside." And going to the curtain, he pulled the cord.

The woman was still there! Her eyes were wide and staring as she pressed against the glass. But her fingers no longer scratched. She didn't move. And her face was as white as the snow that had drifted on top of her.

Suddenly Peter realized that this was a real person! He and his friends had been so scared by a make-believe story that they had left an old woman trapped in a snowdrift!

The other boys were thinking the same terrible thoughts. Was she dead? Was there still a chance of saving her? "Help me get her in!" cried Peter, lifting the latch on the bay window and yanking it open.

What seemed like a ton of snow fell in upon the boys. But where was the old woman? They reached through the window, but their searching hands couldn't find her.

"Quick!" cried Peter, dashing out of the room and

down the hall to a door that led to the garage. "Grab the shovels in there!"

The boys had to push hard to get out of the house because of all the snow piled up outside. In some places it was over their heads. But they made their way to the big drift against the bay window and fell to work.

"Don't stop!" cried Peter. "Dig harder! Dig faster!"

Their shovels made the snow fly. The mound got lower and lower until they were scraping the ground.

"I can't believe this," Gonzo panted breathlessly. "She has to be here. I saw her!"

"Me too," gasped Billy, wiping snow from his mouth and eyes. "But maybe she got out of it by herself and she's all right!"

"You think it's possible?" asked Peter.

Just then Mrs. Cabot came to the door. "I'm glad to see you're all playing instead of scaring yourselves silly. Now come in for breakfast."

The confused boys went back inside the house, shaking off snow, and sat down to eat.

"Brrr!" said Peter's mother after a while. "The heat's been back on for hours. So why is the house still so cold?"

"I guess it's because we opened the window in the playroom," mumbled Peter dully.

"That was intelligent," declared Mr. Cabot. "What would you say to closing it?"

Peter said nothing. He just sat there.

"Come on, son," his dad added more softly. "You can't still be afraid of that ghost looking in at you."

There was no use explaining. Getting up quietly, Peter went to close the bay window.

It was only after he had shut it that he began to have a very strange feeling. It started with a tingling in his skin—and a weird sensation that there was someone else in the room.

He looked around and saw nothing, nothing but the chunks of snow that had fallen in. But as he started to leave, he felt an icy breath of air against his face.

And the voice of an old woman murmured softly in his ear, "Thank thee for letting me in! Now we shall dwell here together."

THE SUBSTITUTE TEACHER

I have heard all about this class," said the substitute teacher as the children took their seats. "I know the tricks you pull and how wild you can be. Yes, I know everything about you."

She paused to glare from face to face with eyes that were dark and staring. "And don't you imagine for one moment that I don't know what's inside your little heads right now. You think that because your real teacher isn't here today—and because this is April First—you can get away with anything. Well, let me tell you that you are very much mistaken, because you know nothing about *me*. I will begin by saying that I am not what I seem to be. I am not a young woman about the age of your mothers and fathers. No, I was born long before even your grandparents were. And I died many years before any one of you came into this world."

Although it was a warm day and the windows were closed, a shiver ran through the class. The substitute noticed it and grinned. Then she went on.

"You may well wonder how the dead can be brought back to life. I will tell you how I managed to do it for myself.

"When I was young I studied the arts of magic. I learned how to keep dead bodies from becoming food for worms. Then, on the night before I took my last breath, I drank the witch's potion I had brewed. It could not keep me from dying, but it saved my corpse."

She paused for a moment, stood up, and smiled evilly. "I look pretty good, wouldn't you say, children, for a dead person?"

No one spoke. No one dared to. They were all too terrified. The substitute sat down again and continued.

"For many, many years I lay dead in my coffin, waiting for life to come back into my body. But something was needed to make me stir again. A great shock of some kind that would make the earth heave and rocks split open." She smiled again. "Of course, you all know about the earthquake in San Francisco, California, a few years ago, don't you? Answer me!"

The shaking children nodded their heads.

"My grave was right where it happened. The earth shook, rumbled, and shifted. The energy of that quake poured new life back into me. I had such strength that I pushed upon the lid of my coffin and flung off the earth above it. But I did nothing then. No, no. I waited until all was calm again. Then, quietly, in the darkness, I slipped out of the coffin and left the graveyard.

"I went wandering through the city. Everything had changed so much since the day I'd died that I did not recognize anything. No one traveled in carriages pulled by horses. Instead there were machines to take them wherever they wanted to go. There were machines in the sky instead of birds. The houses were lit by electricity. And there were more people on the streets than I had ever seen in one place before.

"I did not like all this rushing about . . . all this noise. Oh, how I longed for those peaceful days before I died! My footsteps took me back to the cemetery. Then I saw that I was not the only dead person in the same condition. There were others like myself walking about. But they had not drunk the magic potion and been properly preserved. The worms had eaten most of their brains. They were only walking zombies, mindless creatures, unable to think."

Once again, the teacher paused and gazed around the room. "But there was among these living dead someone whom I recognized from the good old days. Like myself, she had practiced the magical arts. She, too, had kept her brains. By some miracle, she had in fact come back to life ten years before I did. And now she came looking for me. How glad we were to see each other—your regular teacher and I!"

The children turned, wide-eyed, to each other, and the substitute cackled.

"Ha, ha, ha! Yes, she was your Miss Simmons! She took me to her home and let me stay in her guest room. She told me about all sorts of things, especially what it was like to teach a class.

" 'I have fourth graders,' she said. 'But they aren't like children used to be. They aren't all well-behaved. When they don't want to do what you tell them, they talk back to you.'

" 'You mean even after you spank them?' I asked in amazement.

" 'Oh, we are not allowed to spank children,' your teacher said. 'If I did that I would lose my job. And the children know it!'

" 'Scandalous!' I said. 'But there's another solution, of course. Just put a curse on any child who's disobedient. I'm sure you still know how to turn anyone you wish into a frog or a mouse or some other tiny creature.'

" 'In the old days I would have,' she said. 'But I've grown so soft-hearted that I just can't bring myself to do it anymore.' Your teacher fell silent. Then she said to me, 'I wonder if I could ask you for a tremendous favor. You used to teach. You could become a substitute teacher. If things get too trying for me, well then, I'll just play sick one day, and you can take my place. Then the students are all yours! You can do anything you want!'

" 'Sounds good,' I said. 'But I'll need a list of all the students who've given you trouble.' "

The substitute teacher held up a sheet of paper with writing on it. Then she walked to the blackboard and picked up a piece of chalk. "I want each boy or girl whose name I write on the board to stand up and choose whether to become a frog or a mouse. I am afraid that's the best I can do for you."

She started to write the first name. Then she stopped. "I'm hearing a lot of quaking and shaking, but is there anyone who has anything to say?" The substitute turned around, her eyes flashing. "If so, raise your hand!"

The kids sat there, gripping their desks.

"Well," she said, "then I've got something *I* want to say.

"APRIL FOOL!"

THE TONGUE OF FRANKENSTEIN

T he Monster had been destroyed. The scientist who had made the creature was dead. A whole month had gone by, but the people of the village were still afraid. There was no one who dared to set foot in the laboratory of the mad doctor Victor Frankenstein.

No one, that is, but a mere boy. His name was Hans. And he liked to do things that others would not dare to dream of.

So one day he went up the mountain road to the gloomy castle at the top and turned the knob of the great door. It creaked open and he stepped inside.

The machinery for creating life from death was still there. But lightning had come through an opening high up in the roof and smashed all of it to pieces. The only things left unbroken in the laboratory were a low table— and the huge glass bowl on top of it.

The bowl was filled with water that was a strange reddish color. Floating in it was a large human tongue.

As Hans looked, a very strange thing happened. The tongue began to move around the bowl as if it was swimming. Faster and faster it went until the water began to splash. Then it lifted itself halfway out and called, "Me need SEE!"

The boy was no coward, but he ran from the lab in terror. He was halfway down the mountain before a thought came into his head that brought him to a stop. "Wait a minute," he said to himself. "What I just saw was one of Dr. Frankenstein's experiments. If I finish it myself, I might become famous!"

Hans went down to the shore of a nearby lake and waited for the fishermen to come in with their catch. The few coins in his pocket were enough to buy a fish with large, staring eyes. Carefully, when no one was watching, he popped out the eyeballs and hurried back to the lab.

Hans dropped the eyes into the bowl and waited to see what would happen. At first they just bobbed and floated by themselves. But then they drew together. They turned together. And they stared at Hans.

Hans didn't like the way they were looking at him, and he started to think of leaving. Suddenly the tongue swam between the eyes, and they all began to move around the bowl together. Picking up speed, the tongue leaped into the air, crying, "Me need TOUCH!"

"But where am I going to get a hand?" Hans asked in alarm.

There was no answer, of course, for the bowl lacked an ear. But Hans already had an idea. That evening he rode his father's horse to the nearest city. His older brother Fritz was studying to become a doctor there.

Hans found Fritz in his room near the medical school, and he told him what he needed and why. "I know you have to cut up dead people to see what their insides are like," said Hans. "I'll never ask another favor of you if you help me now. Tomorrow I'll bring the hand right back. You can sew it on again and no one will know the difference! This is for science, Fritz. And to make me famous!"

"Are you insane?" exclaimed his brother. "I'm not going to lend you a hand for something like this! Stay away from that place."

But Hans wouldn't listen. Sneaking into the medical school with a knife, he found where the corpses were kept and went to work.

As soon as he was done, Hans galloped back to the village. He climbed the mountain road and ran into the lab. "Here you are. A hand!" he said proudly, and let it fall into the reddish water. Then he stepped back and waited.

But nothing happened. The hand just lay at the bottom of the huge bowl and didn't stir. Finally the tongue swam up to the hand and slowly started to lick it. Then the fish eyes came up close to it and stared so hard that they began to glow. At last the fingers began to move.

The tongue began to circle the bowl until suddenly it leaped for joy. "Got SECRET!" it cried, and fell back into the water.

The boy wanted to hear the secret, but the tongue seemed to be tired now. All it could do was swim slowly and lift itself only a little bit out of the water. When it spoke again, it was so softly that Hans couldn't hear what it was trying to say. So he went up to the bowl and lowered his head close to the water.

The hand sprang up and grabbed him by the throat! Hans gave a choking sound as it pulled him toward the water. Then the tongue leaped into the air, shrieking, "Me need BODY!"

TWIN MADNESS

I think all of us know that what they call "brotherly love" doesn't always work out too well. Take the case of Sherman and Herman from my own hometown. They were twins, and when you looked at them it was like seeing double. But they didn't like each other much. Actually, that's putting it nicely. The truth is, these two grown men hated each other right down to their shoes and socks.

Still, the brothers lived in the same house. Their folks had owned it, and now with their parents dead, neither brother was going to let the other brother have it.

Sherman considered himself to be the older of the two. It was only because he'd been born five minutes earlier, but he still thought that entitled him to feel more important. He'd tell everyone that Herman had been born by mistake. His mother, he said, had only intended to have one child. It was as if she had stuttered over a word and said the same thing twice when she only meant to say it once.

Herman got even for all of this in his own sweet way. He knew how much Sherman hated cats. So every time he'd go down to the big city, he'd look around until he found some stray cat in an alley and then bring it back home to the farm.

That old house was full of alley cats. They yowled all night and climbed all over everything. And with so many of them in one place, they sometimes missed making their deposits in the kitty litter box by a country mile. Then they scratched up the nice furniture that Herman's brother liked to bring back from auctions and garage sales. All in all, they made Sherman's life a misery. And that, of course, made Herman love those cats even more.

One day Sherman decided he couldn't take it any

longer. When his brother was away at the county fair, he drove a rented truck up to the house. He opened the front door and laid down a trail of catnip that led into the back of the truck. As soon as all of the cats had run inside to have a party, he slammed that truck gate shut and drove away.

Now, Sherman wasn't a bad-hearted fellow, except when it came to his twin brother. So he drove up and down the roads until he found good homes for all the cats. Then he went back to his place and started to clean the house.

He went over that place from top to bottom. He aired out the rooms and scrubbed everything clean and mended what had been torn. Pretty soon there wasn't even a smell to remember those kitties by.

Then Herman came home. And the first thing he did was sniff the air. "Something's wrong in here," he announced right away. But he couldn't figure out what it was. Then he began to set out food for the cats. But none of them showed up to eat it.

"Now what's going on?" he demanded.

"Why, nothing, except that they're all dead," declared Sherman in a pleasant voice.

"Dead?"

"Yep. I drowned 'em all," said Sherman proudly.

"You did what?"

"Stuffed them in some potato sacks and took 'em down to the river and flung 'em in. They floated awhile and scratched to get out a lot. But I threw some rocks at them until they went under."

"YOU KILLED MY CATS?"

"Happiest day of my life," said Sherman.

Now, I don't know if what happened after that was because Herman's mind fell apart, or he just decided to drive his look-alike brother crazy. Maybe it was a little of both. But anyway, Herman began to act a lot less like a person and a lot more like a cat.

He let his nails grow long. His hair, too. He stopped walking on two feet. Everything he did now was on all fours. And sometimes you could hear a low, angry, catlike growl coming from deep inside his throat. And he took to cleaning himself with his tongue—you know, licking his arms and hands. He wouldn't just get up on the sofa, either. No, sir. He'd spring up on it from the floor and start scratching at the upholstery.

Sherman tried to ignore all this, but it was hard. The worst was at night, because no sooner would Sherman fall asleep, than Herman would try to jump up on top of his head. If Sherman pushed him off, Herman would scratch at him or even bite him.

"You keep this up and I'm gonna have them haul you off to the booby hatch," Sherman would threaten. But Herman would only curl up his back and hiss at him. And his eyes would turn yellow.

Sherman went to see a lawyer. "Can you get my brother out of the house?" he pleaded.

The lawyer shook his head. "He owns it, too. Maybe you ought to think about moving out yourself."

"Not me!" cried Sherman. "Two of us can play that game!"

Sherman stopped at the butcher shop on his way home and bought some bones. He put them on the floor of his kitchen, got down on his stomach, and started to gnaw at them.

"Meow," growled Herman suspiciously. "What do you think you're doing?"

"RRRRRRRUFFFF!" Sherman barked at him. He showed his teeth and began to snarl.

Herman's hair rose up on his head and he jumped onto the kitchen table. When Sherman tried to snap at him, Herman swiped at him with his fingernail claws.

That was the start of the yipping and the spitting, the biting and the screeching. And it goes on to this very day.

We neighbors can't stand all the racket they make. Tonight we are holding a meeting about it. We'll all have to decide whether to call the police to arrest them . . . or the keepers of the insane asylum to put them in straitjackets . . . or the animal catcher to cart them off to the pound.

I was asked to make a report. So today I snuck up to one of their windows and had a look inside. The house is a wreck of course. Everything is broken. But that's not the worst of it.

You wouldn't recognize Herman and Sherman. They've changed. They don't even look like human beings. To tell you the truth, I don't think they are human anymore.

You know what? I'm beginning to think that maybe it isn't enough to be born human. Maybe you have to want to *stay* human.

Believe me, something horrible happens to folks who spend all their time fighting like cats and dogs!

THE PHANTOM OF HALLOWEEN

The doctors talked excitedly as they took seats in the auditorium. The great Professor Lafarge herself was about to show them a method she had just invented for looking into the minds of the insane. She was already on the stage, standing under a large movie screen. Beside her was a young man who sat like a statue in a wheelchair. There was a metal helmet on top of his head. Wires ran from it to a strange-looking box.

The professor waited for silence. Then she began. "This is a patient who no longer can speak or hear or see, or even feel the jab of a pin. Yet there is nothing wrong with his body. The problem is all in his mind. Some horrible experience has captured his brain and will not let go. He keeps seeing what happened to him over and over. There is no room left for anything else. The police found him in this condition eight years ago today. Now, for the very first time, you and I together are going to discover exactly what that experience was. There is no other way to help him."

The doctors murmured among themselves, and a hand was raised. "Excuse me, Professor, but I don't understand. You just said a moment ago that this man doesn't speak."

Professor Lafarge smiled. "That is exactly what the helmet I have placed on his head is for. It will pick up the electrical waves made by his brain and send them to the box I call the Translator. This device will turn those waves back into the same images, sounds, and thoughts that are running in his own mind. Then it will project them onto that movie screen."

The professor walked to the box and began to inspect the controls. "I am waiting for a red light to go on. That will be the signal that he has come to the end of his experience and is about to begin it again. Ah, there it is."

Professor Lafarge flipped the switch that started the experiment. When the screen lit up, the audience saw the same young man walking into a newspaper office.

"Willy, I want to talk to you," called his editor from behind a large desk.

The young man took a seat. "What's up, Chief?"

"Nothing much, and that's the problem," said the editor glumly. "We need a good story for tomorrow's edition. Look, tonight is Halloween. Why don't you pick some small town where the kids still make a big deal about it and see what you can come back with."

"Oh, come on, Chief," complained Willy. "That's a lousy assignment. The small kids become bunnies and monsters and go knocking on doors. The bigger ones zap each other with shaving cream. And the teenagers show off. It's the same old stuff we used to do. Who cares?"

The editor leaned across his desk. "That's the wrong attitude, Willy. A real reporter keeps digging until he finds a good story."

"Okay, okay. I'll come back with one that'll blow you right out of your seat!" Willy grabbed a camera and left the office with his face burning.

That evening he drove to a little town in the nearby mountains. He parked the car and started walking around the main square, where the stores had stayed open late. Dozens of children in costumes were running in and out, yelling "Trick or treat!" and collecting candy.

Willy snapped a few pleasant pictures as he went along. But he was discouraged. "What have I got to write about that's news?" he asked himself. "I've got to find something different. Something unusual!"

Leaving the square, he turned onto one of the side streets. There were children here, too—young ones who ran in packs ahead of their parents to the houses of people they already knew. Kindly folks came to the doors with big smiles on their faces and lots of treats to give out.

Willy snapped a few more pictures. But finding a good story here was something else. "Looks like all I'm going to get out of this is a cold," he said to himself, pulling his coat tighter.

Just then, far ahead, something flitted across the street. It was gone behind a house so quickly that Willy wasn't sure what he had seen. Then he saw it again in the moonlight as it flitted back across the road toward another house—a figure in a black cape, robe, and hood. The figure of a man.

He's probably just going to a Halloween party and trying to find the right address, thought Willy. *But what the heck, I might as well check this out.*

As he walked up the street, Willy noticed how quiet and dark everything was. There was not a single child here going from door to door. There were no lights in any of the windows. Even the sky seemed to be blotted out by the huge trees that grew high above the houses.

What was this character in a hood and cape doing? the reporter wondered. He certainly wasn't going to any costume party here. Willy watched him dart like a phantom from the shadow of one tree to another.

"The guy must be trying to keep from being seen in the moonlight," Willy said to himself. "But why? Is he looking for a place to rob?"

Somehow that didn't seem to be it. While the man would sneak up to one house after another, he never went close to any of the windows. He would just stare at each house, as if trying to make up his mind about something. Then he'd move on.

"So he's not a burglar," the reporter said to himself. "Then what is he?"

Until then, Willy had also been very careful about not being seen or heard as he followed the man he hoped to write about. But now the hooded figure turned his head and was starting to look at *him*.

Willy ducked behind a parked car, but it was too late. The phantom raised a fist at him, then broke into a run and vanished from sight in a grove of trees.

Fist or no fist, here was real news—and Willy meant to get it! Plunging into the woods, he ran until he saw a stone fence. The phantom stood on top of it, his arms and cape spread out in the moonlight like wings. Then he dropped to the other side and was gone. Willy sprang to the fence and threw himself over it.

Suddenly he was in a cemetery. "I'm chasing a weirdo, and I don't even like graveyards when it's daytime!" Willy said to himself. "But I've gone this far. I can't chicken out now."

But where had the guy disappeared to? Swallowing his fears, Willy began looking around among the gravestones.

The moon slipped behind some clouds. The cemetery was very dark. But the October wind carried the sound of running feet.

And there was the phantom, his dark shape fleeing through the open gates of the cemetery.

Willy ran after him, shouting, "Wait a minute, will you, please! I only want to talk to you. Wait up."

All at once the phantom was gone. Willy found himself standing in front of an abandoned church. The heavy door was hanging loose on broken hinges. The stained-glass windows had long ago been smashed into gaping holes. Wind blew through the old building, shaking the cobwebs inside.

As Willy entered the church, he heard a deep, sad voice rumble in the gloom, "Why are you following me?"

"I don't mean you any harm," said Willy. "You seem interesting, that's all. I'm only a reporter looking for a Halloween story. Human interest, you know."

"For you there can be no story. You have not been

selected," rumbled the phantom voice gravely.

"Selected for what?"

"That I cannot tell you. But you do not know how fortunate you are. Now get away from me, quickly!"

"Okay, no problem," said Willy, backing away. "You don't have to say it twice. Look, I'm taking off."

Leaving the church, Willy walked down to where the road curved. Then he ducked into the bushes to wait. "I must be nuts to do this," he told himself. "But a story is a story."

It wasn't long before he heard footsteps on the path. The hooded man came down the road—and stopped three feet away from the bush where Willy was crouching.

"I know you are there," said the phantom wearily. "I had thought that on this night of all nights I could go about my business just the way I am and nobody would even notice me. But you have refused to leave me alone!"

He began to push back his hood. "Look then," he said as he slowly turned toward Willy. "Look into *madness*."

Willy stared at what should have been a face. But there was nothing except a vast black hole that grew larger and larger. It seemed to take a deep breath—and all at once the breeze behind Willy grew stronger and began rushing into the hole. The howling wind became a hurricane that pushed him toward the ever widening pit. He tried to fight it, but he couldn't. Darkness came over his eyes. He was falling—into the pit!

Willy screamed as he plunged, but there was no sound. He stared, but there was nothing to see. He reached out, but he could not touch anything.

Where was he? What had happened? His mind was beginning to grow as dark as the blackness all around him. He had to remember! If he couldn't remember, then how could he even try to get out?

Little by little his memory started to come back. Yes, that was it! Everything had started when he'd gone into the newspaper office to see his editor, and . . .

Eight years later, in the auditorium, Professor Lafarge was also trying to remember what she had just seen on the movie screen. So were all the doctors in the audience.

They could think of nothing else. They felt as if they were falling. They had to try to figure out why. They had to try to remember.

And they had to get back!

At first their bulging eyes stared at the screen. But soon there was no need to. Everything that was playing on it would also be playing over and over and over—in their own minds.

THE VIPER IS COMING

Sara could tell she was in trouble when her big brother started punching his catcher's mitt. "Why do I have to stay home and watch her?" he bellowed at their mother for the tenth time.

"I'm not going to repeat myself anymore," Mrs. Ross declared as she quickly headed for the front door in her nurse's uniform. "What I want is for everyone to do their part around here."

"I am doing my part," Paul cried, hurrying out of the house after her. "But why can't I go to my game and take Sara with me?"

"I've already answered that, too."

"But the little brat isn't sick anymore! You said her fever is down!"

"Please don't give me medical advice," snapped their mother as she got into her car. "And your sister is not a little brat. Don't you dare take it out on her that I suddenly got called back to work! In case you've forgotten, young man, keeping my job is how I feed this family!" The car door slammed and she drove away.

"I'm sorry you're missing your game," Sara called honestly. "And I *told* Mommy I'd be all right if she let me go with you."

"Yeah, sure," Paul grunted, heading back into the house. "I saw how hard you tried to convince her."

He wouldn't even look at her, but she followed him to the living room. "We could have fun here, Paul. Let's play something."

"Don't wanna play something." He went to the shelf where his collection of videos was kept. "I wanna watch something."

Sara stopped by the rocker. "Can I watch, too?"

"Suit yourself. But I'm warning you, I'm in the mood for blood and gore."

"Can't we . . . can't we watch something nice?" Sara sat down on the edge of the chair, just in case she had to jump right up again.

"Nice?" Paul snickered. Shoving the video he'd picked into the VCR, he threw himself onto the sofa, pressing buttons on the remote control.

The screen was snowy at first. Suddenly, across the screen came the words:

THE BLOODY AXE MURDERS

"Paul, no! Not that one!" cried Sara, covering her eyes. "I'll have nightmares!"

"Oh, for crying out loud," he snorted. "Nobody's even been hacked to pieces yet!"

"Can't you *please* play something else?"

"Nobody told you you have to watch, Sara."

"But I'll hear it!"

"Not if you go somewhere else and don't listen!"

"But I'll know it's on!"

"All right. All right!" Paul got up and stopped the movie. "Here, we'll watch *Dracula*. Even the littlest scaredy-cat won't be bothered by a vampire bat that flies into people's rooms at night and—"

"Don't tell me about it!" Sara jumped to her feet and ran out of the room.

Paul chased after her, a wicked grin on his face. "Will you stop being such a baby? Let me tell you the story. You'll see, it's not really scary at all. Dracula is neither alive nor dead, see? He's got these two long, sharp teeth. He needs them because he's got to find blood to drink. But it has to be the blood of someone who's living."

Sara covered her ears and ran to the stairs, screaming, "Leave me alone. Leave me alone!"

But Paul shouted louder. "Dracula waits until you're asleep. Then he sinks his two long fangs into your neck. But if he likes you he won't drink all of your blood. Just enough to turn you into a vampire like him. Then you get to sleep in a coffin and—"

Sara turned on him suddenly. "Paul," she cried, trying hard to sound just like her mother, "you're being obnoxious!"

"Obnoxious" was a word that Paul couldn't stand. "You're just trying to bug me," he growled. "You don't even know what 'obnoxious' means."

"Yes, I do."

"Oh yeah? What?"

"It means you're a jerk!"

"You get outta my way!" Paul shouted as he shoved past her and slammed into his room. Sara heard him drop onto his bed so hard, it sounded as if the boards under the mattress might break. A moment later, his radio began to blast.

Sara went into her own room, thinking about what had happened. Well, he had tried to scare her, but she'd stopped him. It made her feel like a strong person. But she also remembered how much Paul had been looking forward to playing with his team. That made it hard to stay angry with him. Besides, her mother had quietly told her more than once not to pay too much attention to the way Paul had been acting lately.

"Your brother is having a tough time growing up," she'd said. "Especially without his dad around."

Paul would probably yell "Get lost!" at her if she tried to make up with him. But Sara went back anyway and knocked on his door. When he didn't answer after a few tries, she gave up.

"Some big brother!" she muttered. "A big brother who pouts!" Stomping back to her room, Sara got out her all-time favorite book and sat down to reread it.

But the music coming from Paul's room was so loud that it shook the floor. Finally she went back to his door, calling, "I won't bother you anymore, but could you turn the music down, please?"

There was no reply.

Sara began to wonder if Paul was even in there. Maybe he'd gotten so mad that he'd sneaked out of the house and left her here alone! Getting down on the carpet, she tried to look underneath the door. But she couldn't see anything. She stood up and carefully tried the knob. The door wasn't locked. Fearful that Paul was just waiting on the other side to throw something at her, she opened it slowly. His room was empty!

No sooner did Sara turn off his radio than she heard the telephone ringing. The upstairs phone was in her mother's room. Rushing to it, she snapped up the receiver, saying, "Paul, this isn't funny!"

"Who . . . is . . . Paul?" hissed a low voice. "I am the Viper! And in half an hour exactly I come to your house!"

That was all she heard before the phone went dead.

The man's voice had scared her. And so did that terrible-sounding word. Sara repeated it to herself. "Viper?" What did it mean? There was a dictionary next to her mother's book of crossword puzzles. It told her a viper is a kind of poisonous snake.

"Oh no!" Was this somebody who thought he was a snake? Was a crazy person coming to the house while she was all alone? Where was her brother when she needed him?

Suddenly she remembered how angry Paul had been, and how much he had already tried to scare her.

"How silly I'm being," Sara told herself. "Paul's changed his voice, that's all. He's calling from a friend's house, and he's trying to scare me to death. Well, I'm not the big baby he thinks I am!"

Still, Sara was feeling shaky. This was the first time she'd ever been left in the house by herself. Hurrying to the kitchen, she poured herself a big glass of milk. It helped to calm her a little. She was just cleaning up when the phone rang again.

"This is the Viper," warned the same voice. "Ten minutes more and for sure I come to your house!" Then he hung up again.

44

By now Sara had an idea of what her brother was planning to do. One night, Paul had climbed into the house through her window, pretending he was the Tooth Fairy. That had been all right, sort of, because he hadn't really meant to scare her.

"But this time," she told herself, "he'll probably fix himself up to look like some monster from one of those horrible movies!"

Well, Paul was not going to get away with it! Rushing back to the kitchen, Sara climbed on a chair and took down three boxes of chocolate pudding mix. Quickly ripping them open, she dumped the powder into a bucket. Then she poured some milk and a lot of warm water on top of it. She added ketchup. And fruit juice. Then she stuck her arms deep into the garbage and pulled out banana peels and the slimiest leaves of lettuce she could find. Sara used the handle of a broom to stir the whole mess into a thick, disgusting syrup.

It was a hard job dragging that heavy load up the stairs without spilling anything. And it was just as hard to stand the bucket up on the sill of her open window.

The ten minutes were almost up. Now the phone rang again. "This is the Viper," declared the caller. "Now I come straight to your house!"

Another thought popped into Sara's head. "What if he tries to get in a different way?" As fast as she could, she dashed from one room to another and locked the windows, then down the stairs to put chains on the doors.

Breathlessly, she raced back to her own room—just in time to hear dragging footsteps on the path below. Sara's heart beat faster. There was a little thud against the side of the house as the top of the ladder came to rest just beneath her window. Then she heard heavy breathing and climbing feet hitting the metal rungs of the ladder.

Biting her lip in excitement, Sara waited until she saw fingers reaching out for the top of the ladder. "Now!" she told herself, and tipped the bucket over. The thick, slippery goop rolled out of the bucket and splashed down over the fingers and onto the person below. He let out a terrible yowl, and down to the ground he tumbled.

"Paul," she called out after him. "Don't ever try to scare me again!"

"I won't, sis, I promise," a familiar voice behind her said. "And I'm sorry for the way I—"

Sara whirled around. Her brother was standing in front of her, still holding his catcher's mitt. "Paul!" she gasped. "Then you're not—! Then who—?"

All at once Sara realized the horrible truth. There really was a Viper! And he had just tried to get into the house. Paul was starting to say something about having been up in the attic thinking things over, but she couldn't listen now. All she could think of was that the Viper might be looking for another way to break in and kill them both.

"We've got to get the police!" she screamed, and ran for her mother's room.

Diving across the bed, Sara snapped up the phone. But it was too late to call for help. She must have picked up the receiver just as it was about to ring. The Viper was already on the line. He was coughing and spitting, as if he was trying to get something disgusting out of his mouth.

"PAHH! PITOOEE!" cried the furious voice. "Now you vill be punished for this thing you did to me! You tell your mother that never again vill the Viper come to your house to vipe your vindows!"

THE GOLDEN BROOCH

Ever since his mother had died, little Jamie had had trouble falling asleep at night, even with the hallway light on. He said it was because he was afraid that monsters and other evil creatures might come into his room.

Jamie made up magic chants to keep the monsters

away, but he couldn't be sure they would work. Other times, he was afraid that they might work too well! Then the monsters would give up trying to carry him away and go after his father instead. It all worried him so much that he started sucking his thumb again.

Jamie's dad didn't know what to do about it. But one evening, the boy's grandfather came over to visit. He went into Jamie's room and sat down on the edge of the bed to tell him a story.

"Now, this is going to be a little bit scary for you," old Abraham said gently. "But it might help you to feel less worried about all the terrible things that can happen. I want you to be a brave boy and listen anyway. Will you do that for me?"

Jamie slipped deeper under his blankets and nodded. This is the story Grandpa Abraham told:

Many years ago—before there were automobiles—a young man went riding on his horse. He wandered far from his little town and found himself upon a road he'd never been on before. It twisted and turned and branched off in all sorts of directions. He soon became lost in a wilderness, and night was fast closing in on him.

For a long time the young man—whose name was Jamie, just like you—rode on in darkness. Then he saw a house. But it was a silent, dark, and gloomy place. The wooden shutters on the windows were tightly closed—all, that is, but the one in the attic. And behind its glass, someone whose face he could not make out was staring down at him.

"Hello," Jamie called. "I'm a stranger here, and I've lost my way. Can you help me, please?"

A candle flared in the blackness of the room. The window opened and a young woman looked out. She had long, flowing black hair, eyes that were large and gentle, and a face that beamed like the moon. To Jamie, she seemed so beautiful that it took him a moment or two to remember why he had called out to her.

"Ex...excuse me," he stammered in embarrassment. "Can you tell me the way back to town?"

"That way," she said in a voice as soft as rose petals falling. "Just keep following the stream."

Jamie thanked her, but he didn't want to leave. He rode back to town with an aching feeling in his chest. He knew that it would never go away until he saw her again.

Jamie had to work all the next day, making jewelry in his father's goldsmith shop. But in the evening, he rode out again, following the winding stream until he came back to the part of the woods where he had seen the beautiful woman.

But where had the house gone? It seemed to have vanished. Jamie wondered if he had made a mistake. Perhaps this was a different road altogether. But he could not give up now. He had to find her!

Jamie rode on and on. At last, he came to a little bridge. Just on the other side of it was the house! But this time there was a shutter across the attic window. And though he cried, "Hello. I've come back," it did not open. The woman did not appear.

Climbing down from his horse, Jamie knocked on the door. No one answered. He rapped again, harder this time. Finally the door creaked open, and the face of an old woman appeared.

Now, there's many an old lady who is a wonder to see. All her wrinkles and lines are really like the book of her life, and you can see the gentleness and the love and the good feelings that are part of her. But this woman was a wicked person. All her years had only made her meaner, and that's what you could see in her face. She was holding a thick wooden cane that was twisted like a snake and had a snake's skull for a handle. But she didn't use it to help her walk. No, it was to wave in the face of anyone who bothered her.

"What do you want?" she snapped, lifting the cane as if she was going to hit Jamie with it.

"Please, ma'am," he said. "I mean no one any harm. I would like to speak to the young lady who lives upstairs."

"No one lives upstairs!" screeched the hag. "I am the only one here. Now go away!"

And she slammed the door in his face.

Jamie was confused and very sad as he slowly got

back on his horse. The old woman wasn't telling the truth, but what could he do? He was about to ride away when the shutter over the attic window was flung open.

"I am here!" he heard the girl whisper.

Jamie looked up, but he couldn't see her.

"Where are you?" he called softly. "Light a candle."

"I'm afraid to."

"Just for a moment."

There was flicker of light, and her saw her again. She gazed at him with such fear and sadness that it almost made him cry.

"Are you a prisoner?" he asked, after she quickly put the light out.

"Yes!"

"Climb down and I'll take you away from here."

"Not now. She's old but very fast, and when she rides the wind she'll catch us. Come for me tomorrow night during the storm. When there is thunder and lightning, she will not stir from the house."

Jamie looked at the sky. There was not a cloud in it.

"Trust that what I say is true, beloved. Can you bring a wedding carriage?"

"Yes!" he said. He rode home, bursting with joy because she had called him "beloved" and wanted to be his bride.

All the next day Jamie labored in his father's goldsmith shop making a present for her. From a single bar of shining gold he carved two hearts that were joined together. And when night came he borrowed his father's carriage and hitched the horse to it.

The sky was bright with stars when Jamie set out, but it soon darkened. Lightning flashed, thunder rumbled, and heavy rain began to fall.

The horse did not like the weather and tried to turn back. But Jamie held firm to the reins and drove on until he came to the bridge. Then his heart sank down into his boots.

The house was gone.

"I'll find her!" he promised himself. "I won't stop until I find her!"

He shook the reins hard and sent his horse galloping this way and that. The carriage rolled on and on until the poor animal was stumbling and fighting for breath.

It would have been cruel not to let the exhausted creature rest. Jamie drove under a ledge and stopped the carriage. Then he unhitched the horse and shut his own weary eyes.

Jamie thought he would sleep for only a moment or two, but it was morning before he wakened. The storm was over and the horse was peacefully grazing in the grass. Jamie found some wild berries to eat, then set out again.

For three nights and two days, Jamie searched for the house. But he had no luck at all. By the third evening, the young man was in despair. Would he never find the beautiful woman? he asked himself as he drove along. Would she never be his bride?

Once again, it began to storm. In the light of a thunderbolt, Jamie suddenly saw the house. This time it was perched high on a hill, looking more frightening than ever. But Jamie would not allow himself to be afraid. He wrapped his horse's hoofs in cloth so they would not make a sound when they struck the earth. Then he started up the steep path to the house.

When Jamie arrived, he looked around. No sound could be heard, not even the rumble of distant thunder. The stillness of a graveyard hung about the place and made his heart pound. But the attic shutter was open. "Dearest one," he called out softly.

"Beloved, you have found me!" a voice whispered back.

Jamie had brought a rope with a hook on the end of it. He tossed it up to her, then waited while she fastened it to the sill. It was very dark now, so dark that he could not see her face as she climbed down. But she smelled like flowers. And his heart leaped to see that she wore a wedding gown and veil!

Jamie had driven the carriage right under the attic window. As soon as she sat down beside him, Jamie shook the reins. The horse was as anxious as the two of them to get away from that place. It snorted loudly and galloped off. Soon they were far away.

But the young woman seemed worried. "Please tell me what's troubling you," Jamie said.

She shook her head and did not answer.

"But, dearest," he pleaded, "we mustn't let there be any secrets between us."

"Perhaps it was wrong of me to come to you dressed like this," the woman said in a shy whisper. "It was so wonderful that you rescued me, but maybe you don't want to marry me."

"Yes, I do!" he cried. "I want to be with you always and forever!"

The veil-covered head turned toward him slowly. "Always and forever? Even though you do not know my name?"

"Your name has nothing to do with it!"

"That is where you have made your mistake!" she said in a voice that had changed into an evil cackle.

Jamie turned to stare into the hideous face of the old hag. A wild shriek flew from her withered lips.

Jamie's horse reared up in terror and bolted into the woods. Jamie pulled hard at the reins, but nothing he could do would slow the horse or stop it from slamming the sides of the carriage into trees.

"So you want to be with your dearest one, do you?" the hag screamed in his face. "Well, she died long ago, but I'll be glad to send you to her. Do you know why, young man? Because my name is *Death*!"

Jamie was struck with horror. The carriage was shaking. It felt as if it was about to turn over. His skin crawled and he could think of nothing but escape. But before he could jump from his seat the hag's fingers reached out to touch the back of his hand. A freezing wind shot through his blood. He could not let go of the reins. His body grew cold and began to shudder. He felt that he was turning to ice.

Through chattering teeth, Jamie cried out. "You lie about her being dead. I saw her with my own eyes!"

"You saw only me in disguise!" screeched the hag.

"I don't believe you. I saw someone who is good and wonderful and beautiful and filled with love! I know she's your prisoner. And I want you to set her free!"

"Never! She's mine. And so are you!"

Jamie could not say afterward what made him do what he did next. Using all the strength he could find, he pulled a frozen hand from the reins. Then he slipped the trembling fingers into a pocket and brought out the brooch he had made in his father's shop.

There was a hissing sound as he touched the hag with the brooch, then a burning smell as if she'd been scorched by a steam iron. Before Jamie's eyes, the old hag melted away. In her place sat the girl, her eyes gleaming with love, her face bright with beauty.

"Dearest, you're free!" Jamie cried as he brought the horse and carriage under control.

"Yes, beloved," she said. "I am no longer Death's prisoner."

Jamie wept for joy and reached out to touch her

shining face. But his hand passed through thin air. "I don't understand," he sobbed.

"I am a spirit," explained the girl. "Our hearts can touch each other, but not our hands. Reach out for me always with your heart, Jamie, whenever you need me. That is my dwelling place now. And wherever you go, I shall be watching over you."

Then she vanished.

The room where little Jamie lay in bed had grown quite still. "A penny for your thoughts," his grandfather said gently.

"I don't have any thoughts, Grandpa. I was just wondering what you're turning in your hand."

"Oh, this," said the old man, opening his fist. "This is a little gift my father made long ago, back in the days before there were automobiles. I gave it to your grandmother when we were married. Then it passed down to your mother when she married your father. Now he and I both want you to keep it for the day when you find someone special to love forever."

"But I already have someone I'll love forever," said the little boy.

"Yes, that's true," said Grandpa, leaning over to kiss him good night. "Your dear mother *is* someone you will love forever." And before he left the room, he placed on the pillow a brooch made of gold in the shape of two hearts.

Jamie slept well that night, and every night afterward. He had no more fear of evil creatures lurking in his room. There was no need of magic spells that might or might not work. His mother's heart of gold was joined to his own. And he held them both in the palm of his hand.

DON'T BE SILLY, DARLING

Debra thought she must be going insane. Why else did something keep whispering in her mind that the man she'd married a month ago was a vampire? So her husband's job made him leave their apartment long before sunrise and not return until after dark. So what? So he was gone on weekends, too.

Well, he was trying to make enough money to buy them a house of their own, that's all.

If it hadn't been for the way they'd first met, these crazy fears would never have occurred to her. They'd met at a costume party, and Philip had come dressed as Dracula. He had made silly jokes about wanting to drink her "fresh young blood." After that, all their dates had been at night. They had even gotten married in the nighttime.

It had all seemed like a big joke. But Debra's parents hadn't thought it was funny for them to be acting like two children. Being grown-up and married, they said, was serious business.

Philip had felt he had to prove to them that he didn't spend much time clowning around. He wanted them to know that he was hard at work, day in and day out, putting burglar alarms in houses.

"It's my job to make other people feel safe," he told them with a smile. "So I will certainly take very good care of your daughter."

It was true that Philip was always kind and gentle with her. But lately, Debra had been having terrible nightmares. In her dreams Philip actually was drinking her blood. In the morning she'd rush to the mirror to search for tiny red spots on her neck. Of course there was nothing to see. Then she'd get angry with herself for being so silly.

Yet every night her fears would come back.

But who could she talk to about this wild idea that

was making her so unhappy? Certainly not her mother and father. They had begged her not to marry a man she hardly knew.

Debra decided to see a doctor who dealt with the problems of young couples. After hearing everything she had to say, he told her not to worry. "I think you are feeling bad about not listening to your parents, so you are letting your imagination run away with you. All you have to do is have your husband take you to work with him one day. You'll see where he goes and what he does. That will put your mind at rest about his being some creature out of a horror movie. In real life those demons do not exist."

Debra felt much better. When Philip got up before dawn the next morning, she said, "Darling, please take me with you today."

"It wouldn't be a good idea," he answered gently. "Putting those alarms in is tricky. I really have to give all my attention to what I'm doing."

"But I promise I'll stay out of your way while you're working."

"No, I'm sorry," Philip replied a bit nervously. He looked out the window at the sky. Already it had grown just a little bit lighter. "Listen, I really do have to go."

"Honey, I have an idea," she said brightly. "Call in sick today and stay home with me. It'll be so much fun. Even schoolchildren play hooky sometimes."

"But we're not schoolchildren," he replied softly. "I

know this has been hard for you. But soon it will be over."

Suddenly all of Debra's fears returned. This was the first time she had ever looked really closely at the teeth in Philip's mouth. Two of them seemed longer and sharper than the others. She had to keep herself from trembling when he came over to kiss her cheek.

"Don't wait up for me," he said as he went out the door. "I may be a little later than usual."

Debra couldn't take any more of this. There was no time to dress. She threw on a bathrobe and ran barefoot out of the back door to her own car. By the time she had driven onto the street, Philip was gone. Keeping her headlights off, she turned the next corner and saw his car up ahead.

Debra followed it onto the main highway. Now there was a truck between her car and his. Good! If he looked in his rearview mirror he wouldn't see her.

They drove past the airport and the racetrack and some tall factory buildings. And then they came to an area where there were gravestones on both sides. The graveyard seemed to go on forever.

Finally, Philip turned off onto a road that led right between the graves. Debra's heart was jumping as she followed him. No one, she thought, puts burglar alarms in cemeteries!

When Philip parked his car, Debra stopped her own a distance away. She saw him get out and rush into one of the crypts—a tomb of the dead!

Debra was so upset that she couldn't think any longer about her own safety. She had to know the truth! But when she tried to open the crypt door, the knob wouldn't turn. Philip had locked himself inside!

Debra ran back to her car. "I should drive away from here," she said to herself. "Drive and drive and never see him again!" But somehow she couldn't leave. "I love my husband!" she told herself. "There must be a sensible explanation for all of this!"

So she sat in her car, confused and unable to do anything. Hours passed. She grew hungry and uncomfortable but still she waited. Morning turned into afternoon. Afternoon slipped into evening. And finally the door of the crypt opened.

Philip walked straight to her car. "Why did you follow me?" he demanded.

"I had to."

"You didn't trust me?"

"Philip, I couldn't help it."

"Because I act so strangely?"

"Yes."

"How?"

"Like a . . . a . . ."

"Like a vampire?"

"Yes!"

Philip opened the car door. "Come with me. I want to show you something." He tried to take her by the hand, but she pulled away from him in fear.

"Debra, if you want to save our marriage, let me show you what I've been doing."

"All right," she said shakily, and followed him to the crypt. Slowly he opened the heavy wooden door for her. It was dark as midnight inside. Stepping ahead of Debra, he switched on a lamp. The crypt had a desk and a chair and a typewriter.

"Look at those pages," he said. "That's the book I've been writing about vampires. It means more to me than anything in the world but you. I come here to make it easier to get into the feeling of my story."

She looked at him in amazement. "But, Philip, why didn't you tell me this was what you were doing?"

"Because your parents were against me from the start. I didn't want them to find out that I didn't have a steady job. So I lied. And then it was hard to tell you the truth. Anyway, now you know."

Debra burst into tears. "Oh, darling," she sobbed, "I've been such a fool!"

"Well, it's my fault, too," he said. "I should have been honest from the start."

That night Philip and Debra went out to a Chinese restaurant for a special dinner. And while they were having a wonderful meal, Philip told her the plot of the book he was writing. Actually it was very much like what had happened to the two of them. But the story still didn't have an ending.

They thought about that for a long time. But it wasn't until they got home and were shutting off the bedroom lights that Debra had an idea. "You know what? I think your book should end with the woman's husband actually turning out to be a vampire."

"Great! That's exactly the way I'll finish it," said Philip as he slowly turned to face her.

His lips drew back into a smile and his two fangs grew.

Debra just had time to see them glinting in the dark. But he sank them deep into her neck before she could scream.

THE TELEPHONE
IN THE COFFIN

Miss Ida Dee Rose was the oldest person in all of Georgia. "I just love being alive!" she would tell whoever came to visit or called her on the telephone. "This fast-spinning world of ours is so interesting that I can't wait to see what's going to happen next."

Lately though, she had to watch it all on television. Ever since she had reached the age of 120 it was hard for her to get out of bed. Even lying there tuckered her out very easily. And sometimes she'd fall asleep for days.

One day she woke up while her doctor was bending over her. "I do declare," he said, "I almost thought you had left us forever, Miss Ida Dee."

"Oh my!" gasped the old lady. "Why, I could have been buried alive and woken up in my coffin!"

This thought frightened her so much that the next day she sent for the undertaker. "Build me a coffin as soon as you can with a telephone inside that works. I want to be able to call my nephew to come free me at once."

Her nephew Charles was sitting by her bedside, and she turned to him. "You will do that for me, won't you, dear? You won't waste any time coming to get your old auntie out?"

"Not a single moment!" he promised, taking her hand and kissing it. "You know that I do love you so."

"What a wonderful young man you are," she said, as she patted his head. "Now, if you all don't mind leaving me alone, I think I'll rest."

Charles walked out of his aunt's house. "She calls me young but I'm almost fifty years old! I've thrown away a big part of my life waiting to get my hands on her money, but that woman means to live forever! And she probably will . . . if I don't do something about it."

Charles waited for a night when he knew that his aunt's maid would be away for a few hours. Then he slipped back into her house . . . and picked up a pillow . . . and crept into the old lady's bedroom while she was sleeping.

The maid found Ida Dee the next morning, lying very still in her bed. The doctor came right away. He examined the body carefully. Then he had her taken to the hospital, where he examined her again. At last he called up her nephew. "I'm afraid your aunt has passed away."

"We've thought so before and we were wrong," said Charles. "Are you absolutely sure she's dead?"

The doctor sighed. "No question about it this time, I'm afraid. She was very lucky to have had such a caring relative as you to look after her for so many years."

"Thank you, doctor," replied Charles. "I'm going to miss her very much."

Charles had to pretend to be unhappy during the funeral. But afterward he drove all the way to the city of Atlanta, where nobody knew him. And there he celebrated by going on a shopping spree. He ordered a new car and bought lots of clothes. Now he could have anything he wanted, no matter what the cost!

It was late in the evening when Charles returned to his apartment, loaded down with presents for himself. He was in a wonderful mood. When the phone rang, he answered it without thinking twice.

"I'm still alive!" cried a voice he knew so well. "Oh, Charles, it's so very dark in here! And I'm so frightened! Please come get me out."

"Who is this?" he demanded wildly. "What kind of a sick joke are you trying to play?"

"Charles, wait! Please don't hang up!"

"I *am* hanging up!" he screamed, slamming down the phone.

The call had made him so upset that he hurried out of the house. He didn't come back until many hours later. But he heard the phone ringing even before he opened the door.

"Let it ring!" Charles sneered as he stumbled to his room. "Go on! Go on! Ring your head off!" And flopping down on the bed with all his clothes on, he fell asleep.

But a phone seemed to be ringing through all his dreams. It was still ringing next morning when he opened his eyes. He grabbed the receiver, growling, "Who's making this racket? And what's your problem?"

"I'm Ida Dee Rose. And I want you to keep your promise!"

"I don't have to do anything!" Charles roared, and he slammed down the phone. Then he took it off the hook so it couldn't ring again.

But now he was very frightened.

"How can it possibly be her?" he asked himself. "I pressed the pillow over her face. I made sure that she couldn't breathe. I watched her die!"

Well, whatever was going on, he refused to take any more of it. These calls had to be stopped! Charles went straight to the telephone company and demanded that they change his number right away. "I want this new number kept secret!" he insisted. "I don't want anybody to find out what it is unless I tell them personally!"

But that night, the phone rang again. Charles picked up the receiver and put it to his ear without speaking.

"Charles! Are you there? Your father was my brother's son. I raised you from a boy. I sent you to college. Don't you care for me at all?"

"Leave me alone!" he roared, yanking on the phone with all his strength. It tore out of the wall, and he flung it out of the window.

Charles spent the rest of the night trying to calm down. But his heart still raced and his hands still shook. When he tried to read, the page went blurry in front of his eyes. He took aspirin to stop the banging in his head, but the hours went by and it only got worse.

Then suddenly he heard ringing. But how could that be? There was no phone! Wait! It was only the doorbell. He would have to get rid of whoever was there. Right now he was in no condition to talk to anybody. He went to the peephole and looked through it. A young woman he had never seen before was standing outside.

"What do you want?" Charles barked.

"Excuse me," she replied. "But I live in one of the apartments upstairs. A lady is on my phone who says she's your aunt, Ida Dee Rose. She says that she must talk to you right away, but something has gone wrong with your line. She's waiting for you now. Please come and talk to her."

"That can't be my aunt. My aunt is dead! That's just some crazy person. She was bothering me, too, until I got rid of my phone. And I don't want to talk to her."

"But this is very upsetting to me. I don't know either of you. And I don't think it's fair that I should be stuck in the middle of your problem. Please, please do something so that she won't start calling me back."

"All right. All right! I'll talk to her."

The neighbor thanked him as they went up to her apartment. "Please let me speak to her alone, if you don't mind," he said.

"Of course. I'll just go into another room."

As soon as she had left him by himself, Charles snatched up the phone and whispered furiously, "Now you listen to me. You may sound like Ida Dee Rose, but I can prove you're not my aunt! I have the number of the phone in her coffin. I'm going to call it right now!" He hung up, then dialed at once.

The phone was picked up on the first ring. "Oh, Charles, why are you treating me so? Won't you come for me now?"

"Yes, I'll come for you!" he screamed. "I certainly will come for you!"

Rushing out of the neighbor's apartment and down

the stairs to the street, he jumped into his car and drove to the deserted cemetery. "A shovel! I need a shovel!" He found one leaning against a tree and hurried to the grave.

All the while Charles was digging he kept thinking that maybe the police were playing him for a fool. Someone could have seen to it that his aunt's telephone number would ring somewhere else. Another person could have imitated his aunt's voice. Maybe the police were looking for a way to trap him!

Well, maybe so. But even now he was too smart for them. What did it prove that he was digging up his aunt's grave? Nothing! He could say that he was only trying to find out if she had been buried by mistake! Isn't that just what a very loving nephew would do?

His shovel struck the top of the coffin. Throwing it aside, he brushed away the last clods of dirt.

When he lifted the lid, Aunt Ida Dee was looking at him. Her lips were starting to part. The old hag was alive!

"Oh, Charles," she began to say.

But he didn't want to hear her! No, not ever again! Charles jumped into the grave, took her by the throat, and shook her so hard that the head dropped off and the springs that were inside burst out of it.

Why, this was nothing but a dummy! A dummy being operated by remote control the way a child might work a toy or a VCR. Someone had put it there in place of his dead aunt!

It was such a great joke on him that he began to laugh. He laughed and laughed as the police officers came out of hiding to arrest him for murder. It was a madman's cackle. And it never stopped until the day he died.

THE MISUNDERSTOOD BOY

My parents were freaking out by the time I got home. They came rushing through the front door before I had my bike halfway up the porch steps. "It's three in the morning!" yelled my dad. "We've already called the police, the hospitals, and the morgue."

My mother told him to stop making so much noise because it would wake the neighbors. Then she began to scream at me, too. "Don't think you can explain this away with another one of your stories, Brian! Because you can't!"

Another one of my stories? I thought. *Just because weird things happen to me, everyone thinks I go around telling lies.* Kicking my bike stand down, I headed for the door, trying to avoid trouble. "Look," I said. "I'm really tired, and I'm sure you are, too. Why don't we talk about it in the morning? You know, like three grown-ups."

If a thunderbolt could have come out of my mother's eyes right then, I think she would have zapped me with it. "Stay right there, you rotten kid! You are not one of the grown-ups. And you don't set foot in this house until you tell me where you went and what you were doing."

Rotten kid, I thought. *Great. Some chance they're going to believe anything I say, much less the truth.*

"I'll tell you what," I said. "Why don't you just let me know what my punishment is going to be. Only, if you don't mind, I'd like to hear it sitting down."

I tried to go inside, but my father stepped in my way. "You heard what your mother said. Let's have it. And don't you dare try to work your way out of this one with another of your whoppers."

It was pretty annoying being told to my face what a con artist I am—and not for the first time either. That's just the sort of thing that makes a guy *want* to lie. But what actually happened that night was crazy enough without my exaggerating it.

"Okay." I sighed. "Here goes. It started when I was in my room doing homework and—"

"Homework!" exploded my mother, throwing her arms in the air. "What a joke!"

"But it's true." Which, strangely enough for me, it was.

"That'll be the day," snickered my father.

"I won't argue about it," I muttered, trying real hard to keep my cool. "Anyway, the doorbell rang and I came downstairs to open it. And there was Grandpa."

"Now I know you're lying!" snorted my mother, as if she was happy to catch me at it. "I spoke to my dad on the phone a few hours ago and he was still in Hawaii!"

Let them do all the yelling, I told myself. Quietly, I said, "No, I mean my other grandpa. The one who's in Woodmere Cemetery, only a few miles away. Anyway, I didn't recognize him at first, because he was just a skeleton. He was poking a bone that used to be his finger into the bell."

I stopped for a minute to study their faces. My dad's was getting very red. "I knew you wouldn't believe me."

"Oh, that would be unfair to you, son," he said, meanwhile opening and closing his fists. "Do go on."

"Dad wants to hit me, Mom."

It was just a statement of fact, but my father didn't take it well. "I-do-not-hit!" he hissed at me. "I-never-hit . . . no matter how much I might want to." He turned to my mother. "I am going to give our son enough rope. And then I am going to hang him."

Now that was really great child psychology. I said, "Since you know what a big lie this is, maybe I should just stop now."

"No, you go on," my dad insisted.

"To the bitter end," said my mother. She glared at me. "*Your* bitter end."

I was getting pretty mad myself. But all I did was shrug my shoulders and go on.

"Like I was saying, I didn't know who it was. But even though you grounded me for a week, you've got to remember that tonight was Halloween. So I just figured one of my genius friends had rigged something up. Anyway, the skeleton had this creaky old voice. He said, 'Excuse me, but isn't this the house of Alan and Gloria Rosenkrantz?'

"Well, being stuck in the house hadn't put me in a really good mood, so I said, 'Yeah. So which do you want—a trick or a treat?'

" 'A big hug for your old granddad!' he shouted, and stuck the long white bones of his arms out at me.

"Now, even when it comes to ordinary arms, I think you both know how I don't like getting hugged anymore. Not that either of you has tried recently. Anyway, I wanted to go along with this gag, so I said, 'Grandpa, I'm too old for that now. Let's shake.'

"Which we did. And that's when it happened. His hand broke off."

My dad gave me a funny look. "Fell right off his arm, did it, son?"

"That's right. It did. Even though you don't believe me. Anyway, now I was getting a little bit spooked."

"I can't see why."

"Because it wasn't a plastic hand, like I expected. It was real bones. Then the fingers broke off, too. Right where you're standing. They just came off in my hand and clattered all over the porch."

"This is disgusting!" exclaimed my mother.

"I know, Mom! How do you think I felt? But I couldn't show it, because I realized the skeleton really was Grandpa. And he looked like he was going to cry.

" 'Isn't this terrible!' he said. 'I'm hardly out of my coffin and I'm falling apart already.' "

My dad had been rocking back on his heels. Now he rocked forward till was leaning over me. Then he clamped a hand on my shoulder. "And what did you do to make things right, my boy?"

"Well, I guess I panicked, Dad, because I ran for the glue. But that's absolutely the wrong thing to use, because when you stick a hand back on to the rest of an arm, the wrist gets stiff and doesn't work right. Then the hand can't move anymore.

"I tried not to make the same mistake with the fingers. But it was hard to fit them into the sockets the right way. And if I pushed too hard, Grandpa's whole arm might break right off from his shoulder. Which it did, but only part way."

"That must have aggravated my father's skeleton even more, son."

"Oh no. He told me I did the best I could. But he really felt bad because neither of you were here. And then he started worrying that his other parts would fall off if he waited around till you got back."

"That's perfectly understandable," said my father.

"So I took some glue along, just in case, and brought him back to the cemetery on my bike."

"Well, all of that couldn't have taken you until three in the morning."

Dad was using his extra-soft voice now. That worried me more than being yelled at.

"You are making your father very crazy, Brian," my mother warned me—as if I didn't know that already.

"I'm sorry, Mom. But what can I do? I'm telling the truth."

"Yes, the truth is a wonderful thing," my dad sang out dizzily. "I hope I can still recognize it when I hear it."

"Dad, I'm going to make this short for you, all right?"

"That would be kind of you, my boy." He was staring over my head at the moon. I was beginning to feel sorry for him.

"The whole graveyard was full of other dead people who had come out especially for Halloween. But they were just hanging around, not knowing what to do with themselves. So when they asked me to give them rides on my bike . . ."

"That was the only decent thing to do, wasn't it, son?"

"Look, I know it got very late, but I just couldn't help it. It really cheered Grandpa up! He said he was very proud of me for being so caring. And he thought you and Mom had done a wonderful job of raising me."

"Are you finished now and ready to hear the sentence of the court?" my father demanded.

"Your boy may be ready for it, but I'm not!" cried an angry voice that seemed to be coming from thin air.

It took me a moment to realize what was going on. "Grandpa!" I gasped. "What are you doing here?"

"Well, it was my fault that you got home so late. So I thought I'd sneak back to make sure you didn't get blamed for it. Alan and Gloria, your son is not a liar!"

"Who is speaking?" Dad's eyes zigzagged in every direction. "Who's imitating my father's voice?"

"I'm here in this bag on the back of the bike. Well, not all of me, just my head. If you don't believe that either, then come and take a look."

My folks stared at me wildly. "Brian," yelled my mother, "tell me the truth. Is your grandfather's skull really in there? Or have you suddenly learned how to throw your voice like a ventriloquist?"

"Since you never believe me anyway, I'm going to let

you find out for yourselves," I said with a shrug.

Now they were both trembling too hard to keep me from walking into the house. I don't know which of my parents finally went to look inside the bag. But just as I got to my room, I heard my father begin to beg.

"Come on, Pop, it isn't right for you to come back from the grave. You know it isn't right."

"I'll tell you what isn't right," said Grandpa. "It's the two of you—Brian's own father and mother—refusing to believe every single word of this terrific grandson of mine! Now the both of you are going to shape up real quick. Otherwise you won't be able to get rid of me, even if you try to. I'll get all of my bones together and keep coming back. I'll even bring some of my graveyard friends along. And we'll hide ourselves all over this house. You won't know when or where we'll turn up next. Why, you won't even be able to take a coat off a hanger in peace. Because you could open a door and there I'd be—the skeleton in your closet! Am I making myself clear to you both?"

I heard some gurgling noises, which kind of sounded like my mother and father thinking it over out loud and agreeing to start trusting me.

Well, of course, this wasn't the best way to convince my parents that I wasn't a world-class liar. But who was complaining?

BEST FRIENDS

It was Emma Black's ninety-second birthday. She was feeling a bit tired this morning, not at all like getting out of bed. Perhaps if the rain stopped she might consider going out for a walk later. But it took hours simply to shower and put on all her clothes and be ready to show herself to the world!

Then again, if she didn't go out, what was there to do today? Not very much now that she had trouble reading, even with glasses. And it did feel as if she'd watched enough television to fill five lifetimes.

Emma longed for a good friend to visit with or at least talk to on the phone. But most of those she'd known through the years were gone now. There were so many to miss—one most of all.

Well, these thoughts weren't the best ones to have on her birthday. She was just feeling a little bit lonely, that's all, and sad that there was no one to share her birthday with. But really, wasn't it silly to be sorry for herself when life had been so very good to her?

Suddenly the doorbell rang. "Just a moment," Emma called, reaching for her bathrobe. Slowly she got up, put her feet into her slippers, and went to the door. She opened it only a crack.

There was a boy standing outside. He was dressed like a farmer's son and he had a freckle-faced smile. His face looked familiar somehow. But these days her memory was not always as good as it might be. "Please forgive me, but I'm a mess in the morning. Otherwise, I'd let you in. Can I help you?"

"Happy birthday!" the boy sang out. And his smile grew larger.

"Oh, my goodness! How nice," exclaimed Emma. "Just a moment. Let me take this silly chain off the door. Come in, come in. What is that you have with you? Is that a bicycle built for two? I haven't seen one in ages. Where did you get it?"

"It was my father's."

"Well, it's very nice. But you don't want to get it any wetter than it is. Bring it inside. Just park it here in the hall. Good, good. Why don't you follow me into the kitchen? Do you like milk and cookies?"

"Yes, ma'am," the boy said, following her.

"The milk I'm sure of," she said, going over to the refrigerator as he sat down at the table. "But I don't think I have any cookies."

"That's all right," he said as she came back with the milk carton. "Just milk will be fine."

"Milk without cookies at your age? Nonsense. By the way, what is your age?"

"Eleven, ma'am. But please don't fuss over me."

"But I like to fuss over children! Can't think of a more pleasant thing to do. Why are you grinning at me like that?"

"Well, you like to fuss. And I like to grin."

"What a cheery thing to say! I feel like I know you. Your voice rings as clear as a bell in my head, yet I can't seem to recall where in the world . . . But don't tell me yet who you are. I don't want people to prompt me, you know. It will come. It will come."

Emma thought for a moment. "You can't be one of the children I taught in school. No, I've been retired for so very long. Too long! They're all grown up. You wouldn't by any chance be one of my neighbors, would you?"

"No, ma'am. Not recently." And he smiled at her all the harder.

"Not recently?" The old lady grinned back. "I do believe you're teasing me. Are you?"

"Well, maybe a little."

"You remind me so much of someone," Emma said. "This is so frustrating. I suppose I'm going to have to ask you for a little hint. Tell me your first name."

"My name is Andrew," he said.

"Andrew?" Emma repeated. "I had a friend . . . oh, about eighty years ago, by that name. But everyone called him Andy. Do you ever get called that?"

"Oh sure. Lots of times."

"Well, the Andy that I knew—my Andy—lived on one of the dairy farms out on Bostock Road. We used to be neighbors. And Andy and I . . . we were as close as brother and sister. We did everything together. Helped each other with chores. Played Pocahontas and Captain John Smith. Rode on my father's old plowhorse and pretended he was a camel in the desert. Studied together, too—when you could get us to study. Oh, we had so much fun! And you know, with that smile of yours and those freckles and the way your ears stick out—not too much, but just a little—you do remind me of him."

Emma sighed and closed her eyes, and a little tear ran down her cheek.

"Why are you crying?" the boy asked.

"Well, because . . . because lately I've been missing him more than ever. I think about things from my childhood and how wonderful it was."

She paused to wipe her eyes with a napkin. "You must excuse me. I suppose old people cry too easily." She smiled. "Maybe that's what they really mean when they say that someone is in her second childhood. . . . Anyway, Andy saved my life during a spring flood. There had been a lot of snow that winter, and when it melted it came roaring down the mountain into the creek where I used to go fetch water for the cows. I slipped and fell in. Andy jumped in after me and got me out. But then he was swept under, his head hit a rock, and he drowned. I lost my dearest friend and he lost all these years that could have been his to know and enjoy life."

"What is it you miss about him the most?"

"The most?" she repeated softly. "Well, I suppose it's the wonderful smile that would cover his whole face. It always used to cheer me up when I was feeling blue, like now."

"Wouldn't it be nice," asked the boy, smiling wider than ever, "if you could see him again?"

"Well, I did see him for a long while in my dreams," she sighed. "But as time goes on, you know, people you love who have died stop visiting you."

"Maybe sometimes they can come back in other ways," suggested the boy.

Emma looked up at him. "Wait a moment." Her

eyes opened wide. "Are you trying to tell me . . . ? Are you?"

"Yes, I am!"

"Of course! I should have known right away. You're from the same family! Your parents named you after him. And you found out where I was living and came to see me. How lovely."

"Emma, I wasn't named after him. I am him. It's me! I'm *your* Andy!"

"I don't understand!" Emma cried suddenly, looking up in alarm. "What cruel trick is this to play on an old woman?"

"It's not a trick!"

"It's . . . it's not?" she stuttered. "But if it really is you . . . that means you're a ghost!"

"Yes, and so are you, Emma," he said, standing up. "You've just passed on. I came to tell you not to be afraid, and to take you with me." He put his hand out to her.

"Take me where?"

"I'll show you. That's why I brought my bike."

"But, Andy, I'm much too old to ride on it."

"Not anymore. Just leave your body in the chair and come with me."

When Emma Black sprang to her feet she was a young girl again. She gave Andy her hand—and her best friend led her out of the kitchen and into the hall to the bicycle built for two.

GETTING TO NEW YORK

I t was just a little while ago when it all
happened. We were driving down to New York
City. I had my wife and her sister in the car.
And their annoying old mother, too.

A big summer storm burst right above us just as we
crossed one of the bridges that go over the Hudson

River. When I put on the windshield wipers, they gave a couple of swipes, then stopped working. With all that rain streaming down I had to slow the car and squint to see. Then my mother-in-law piped up with, "A careful person would have double-checked everything in the car before we started out."

Well, I didn't say a word. But my wife could tell that I was burning. "Honey," she said in a low voice. "You'd better pull over and let me drive for a while. You know you get rattled when you're upset."

She was right, of course. But when I get mad I also get stubborn. "Don't you start in on me, too," I grunted. "I'm driving and that's it."

"Watch out!" she screamed.

I don't know exactly how it had happened, but I'd gotten into the wrong lane of traffic. There were cars coming straight at us. I turned the wheel quickly to the right and just barely got out of their way.

We were all pretty shaken up. My wife said, "Why don't we get off this road and stop somewhere until the rain lets up?"

By then I was more than ready to listen to her advice. So I found an exit from the highway and drove slowly into a little town. We pulled into the parking lot of a big hotel and waited until the rain stopped.

I started the car again, and we set out for the highway. But somehow, I just couldn't find it. I made a bunch of turns—and ended up right back in the same hotel parking lot we'd started out from a few minutes earlier!

Just then, I noticed two people walking to a parked car. "Excuse me," I said, rolling down my side window. "Can you tell me which way to go to New York City?"

The man and woman looked at each other, then they stared at me. "Get real!" barked the man. They climbed quickly into their car and drove off.

"What is wrong with those people?" I sputtered. "Talk about nasty!"

My wife patted me gently on the arm. It was her way of reminding me not to lose my temper again.

I nodded and got out of the car. Then I went into the lobby of the hotel and over to the clerk at the front desk. "Hi," I said pleasantly, and the clerk smiled back at me.

"How many are checking in, sir?" he asked politely.

"What? Oh, no, we don't need a room. I seem to be having problems with directions. Could you help me find my way to New York, please?"

The clerk was looking at me strangely now. "That's something you'll have to do for yourself," he said.

"What are you talking about?" I asked him. "Here you are, running a hotel, and you don't know where the biggest city in the country is? It can't be more than thirty or forty miles away! You must have people staying here who go back and forth to New York all the ti—"

He turned away while I was still talking to him.

"I'm sorry, but I'm very busy now," he snapped, and moved to the other end of the desk.

I couldn't believe what had just happened. I walked over to a man who'd been standing near some potted plants with a watering can. He'd been listening and looked as if he might be on my side. "What's the matter with that clerk?" I asked him. "How come he refused to help me?"

"I wouldn't take it personally," the man replied as he sprayed a plant. "It's just the way the rules are."

"Rules? What rules?"

"Some people have to be given a little time before they come around."

"What the heck are you talking about?"

"You just take it easy, and everything will turn out okay." Then he walked away, too.

By now I was so mixed up and confused that I stomped out of that lobby, jumped into my car, and told everyone we'd have to find our way by ourselves.

What a waste of time that turned out to be. The same streets kept twisting and turning and running back into each other. We were driving and driving and not going anywhere!

But then, as we turned the same corner for the fifth or sixth time, I saw a UPS truck parked in front of a store. *UPS*, I thought. *They deliver packages all over the country! We're back in business!*

I pulled over behind the truck and waited on the

sidewalk until the driver came out of the shop. Then I rushed up to him, saying, "Would you do me a big favor, please?"

"I will if I can," he answered.

"Just tell me which way I go to get out of this town and down to New York City."

The driver looked at my car and everyone in it. Then he shook his head. "That question tells me you're not ready yet."

I'd had just about all I could stand of this sort of talk. "What I'm ready for," I shouted at him, "is what people show each other every place but here. A little kindness!"

"If you need a little kindness," said the delivery man as he started walking to his truck, "then stop blaming yourself."

"Blaming myself?" I cried, following him. "Blaming myself for what?"

"You already know the answer to that one," he said, climbing behind the wheel. "But it's so painful that you won't admit it to yourself."

"That's just plain crazy!" I yelled as he started his engine. "Look! All I want is to find out how to get to New York."

"And all I can tell you," the driver called back, "is that there isn't any way to get there from here."

Then he drove off, leaving me standing right here on this sidewalk, trying to figure it out.

And now, as I'm thinking about this, a light is slowly being turned on in my brain. I'm seeing things that I don't want to see. The windshield wipers going off. The rain. Our being in the wrong lane. And those cars driving straight at us.

Now I know why we can't ever get to New York from this place. And it's all my fault. I shouldn't have been driving while I was angry. We are all DEAD!